Mr Gumpy was going for a ride in his car.

He drove out of the gate and down the lane.

"May we come too?" said the children.

"May we?" said the rabbit, the cat, the dog, the pig, the sheep, the chickens, the calf and the goat.

"All right," said Mr Gumpy.
"But it will be a squash."

And they all piled in.

"It's a lovely day," said Mr Gumpy. "Let's take the old cart-track across the fields."

For a while they drove along happily. The sun shone, the engine chugged and everyone was enjoying the ride.

"I don't like the look of those clouds. I think it's going to rain," said Mr Gumpy.

Very soon the dark clouds were right overhead.
Mr Gumpy stopped the car. He jumped out,
put up the hood, and down came the rain.

The road grew muddier and muddier,
and the wheels began to spin.
Mr Gumpy looked at the hill ahead.

"Some of you will have to get out and push,"
he said.

"Not me," said the goat. "I'm too old."

"Not me," said the calf. "I'm too young."

"Not us," said the chickens. "We can't push."

"Not me," said the sheep. "I might catch cold."

"Not me," said the pig.
          "I've a bone in my trotter."

"Not me," said the dog.
          "But I'll drive if you like."

"Not me," said the cat. "It would ruin my fur."

"Not me," said the rabbit. "I'm not very well."

"Not me," said the girl. "He's stronger."

"Not me," said the boy. "She's bigger."

The wheels churned...

The car sank deeper into the mud.
"Now we're really stuck," said Mr Gumpy.
They all got out and pushed.

They pushed and shoved and heaved and strained and gasped and slipped and slithered and squelched.

Slowly the car began to move…

"Don't stop!" cried Mr Gumpy. "Keep it up! We're nearly there."

Everyone gave a mighty heave – the tyres gripped…

The car edged its way to the top of the hill.
They looked up and saw that the sun
was shining.

"We'll drive home across the bridge,"
said Mr Gumpy.
"There'll be time for a swim."

"Goodbye," said Mr Gumpy.
"Come for a drive another day."